Daniel Tries a New Food

Adapted by Becky Friedman
Based on the screenplay written by Becky Friedman
Poses and layouts by Jason Fruchter

Simon Spotlight
New York   London   Toronto   Sydney   New Delhi

SIMON SPOTLIGHT
An imprint of Simon & Schuster Children's Publishing Division
1230 Avenue of the Americas, New York, New York 10020
This Simon Spotlight paperback edition August 2015
© 2015 The Fred Rogers Company
All rights reserved, including the right of reproduction in whole or in part in any form.
SIMON SPOTLIGHT and colophon are registered trademarks of Simon & Schuster, Inc.
For information about special discounts for bulk purchases,
please contact Simon & Schuster Special Sales at 1-866-506-1949 or business@simonandschuster.com.
Manufactured in the United States of America 0716 LAK
10 9 8 7 6 5
ISBN 978-1-4814-4170-4
ISBN 978-1-4814-4171-1 (eBook)

It was a beautiful day in the neighborhood, and Daniel Tiger and Tigey were going on an adventure . . . in the living room.

"Let's go in our cave!" said Daniel.

But when Daniel crept over to the cave, he saw that someone was in his cave! Who was it?

It was Daniel's dad!

"Dad!" Daniel giggled. "What are you doing?"

"I'm not Dad! I'm . . . a silly beast!" said Dad.

"Well, I caught you, you silly beast!" said Daniel, hugging Dad tightly.

Daniel's mom came into the living room. "Daniel, my little adventurer," said Mom, "do you want to help me make something in the kitchen?"

Daniel jumped up happily. "Okay, Mom! I like being a big helper."

In the kitchen Daniel and Mom got ready to cook up a special treat.

"Since Miss Elaina is coming over for dinner tonight, I'm making a new dessert," said Mom. "It's called banana swirl!"

"Banana swirl?" asked Daniel. "What is that?"

"Well, I put these bananas in the freezer," Mom said.

"Brr!" said Daniel. "They're cold!"

"And now we put the bananas in the blender, put the top on, and press . . ."

"GO!" said Daniel, as he pushed the button with Mom.

The bananas swirled around and around in the blender.

"Okay, they're done!" said Mom, as she turned off the blender.

"Wow," said Daniel, "they don't look like bananas anymore."

Mom dipped a spoon into the banana swirl, and held it out to Daniel. "Are you ready to taste?" she asked.

Daniel wasn't sure he wanted to try the banana swirl. "What if I don't like it?" he asked.

"It's true, you might not like it," said Mom. "But it might taste smushy yummy! *Try a new food, it might taste good.*"

"Okay," said Daniel. "I'll try." And very slowly, he took a little bite and . . .

He liked it! "It's swirly, banana-y, it's cold and sweet, and it kind of tastes like banana ice cream!" said Daniel, grinning. "I like banana swirl!"

"I'm glad you tried it," said Mom.

Ding! Dong! The doorbell rang. "Miss Elaina's here!" exclaimed Daniel happily.

Daniel ran to the living room.
"Hiya, toots," said Miss Elaina. "I'm here, and I'm ready to play!"
"I'll call you when dinner is ready," Mom said from the kitchen.
Daniel and Miss Elaina went over to Daniel's cave.

"Let's pretend we're on an adventure," he whispered, "and we're looking for a silly beast!"

"I think I saw a silly beast over there in that cave!" exclaimed Miss Elaina. "It's . . . Tigey!"

That gave Daniel an idea! He imagined that Tigey was a silly beast deep in the jungle.

Dad poked his head into the living room, "Will all silly beasts please come into the kitchen for dinner?"

"Okay!" said Daniel and Miss Elaina.

At the dinner table Mom Tiger was serving spaghetti, but it didn't have the regular tomato sauce on it.

"This is something new," said Mom as she scooped a big helping onto each plate. "It's called veggie spaghetti. These veggies go on top of the spaghetti."

Daniel looked closely at his plate. "I don't think I like veggie spaghetti," he said.

"But, Daniel, you've never tried veggie spaghetti. How do you know that you don't like it?" asked Mom.

Daniel looked at the new food again. "That's true," he said. "I've never tried it." Daniel turned to Miss Elaina, who was about to take a bite. "What do you think, Miss Elaina?"

"Well, toots," said Miss Elaina, "at my house we always say, try a new food, it might taste good!"

Daniel liked it! "It's kind of crunchy and munchy!" Daniel said with a smile. "Veggie spaghetti is good!"
But what about Miss Elaina?

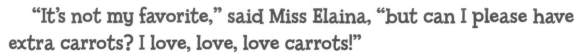

"It's not my favorite," said Miss Elaina, "but can I please have extra carrots? I love, love, love carrots!"

"Absolutely," said Mom Tiger, "and some plain spaghetti, too. I'm glad you both tried something new."

"Me too!" said Daniel, as he finished eating the rest of his veggie spaghetti.

After they finished their dinner, it was time for the special dessert that Daniel and Mom had made together.

"Who wants banana swirl?" asked Mom.

"I do!" said Daniel.

"I do!" said Miss Elaina.

"Banana swirl?" said Dad. "But I've never had banana swirl before. What if I don't like it?"

"Try a new food, it might taste good!" said Daniel and Miss Elaina, giggling.

So Dad took a little bite and . . .

He liked it! "Banana swirl is smushy yummy," said Dad. "I'm glad I tried it."

"Me too!" said Daniel.

I liked trying banana swirl and veggie spaghetti at dinner. Have you ever tried a new food? Try a new food, it might taste good! Ugga Mugga!